Olympic National Park

Touch of the Tide Pool, Crack of the Glacier

Adventures with the Parkers

STORY BY
Mike Graf

ILLUSTRATED BY
Marjorie Leggitt

FULCRUM

Text © 2009 Mike Graf
Illustrations © 2009 Marjorie Leggitt
Photographs © Mike Graf: 11, 12, 14, 15, 17, 20, 24, 33, 41,
49, 54, 55, 59, 64, 72, 74, 75, 84 (top),
© Shutterstock: Cover (all), title page (all), 1, 4–5, 5 (inset), 7,
9, 18–19, 19 (inset), 22–23, 23 (inset), 34–35, 38, 38–39, 39
(inset), 42, 43, 45, 46, 70, 76, 82, 84 (bottom), 86, 88, inside
back cover.
Map courtesy of the National Park Service

Library of Congress Cataloging-in-Publication Data

Graf, Mike.
  Touch of the tide pool, crack of the glacier / by Mike Graf ;
illustrations by Marjorie Leggitt.
     p. cm. -- (Adventures with the Parkers ; v. 5)
  Summary: Twin brother and sister, James and Morgan,
embark on another adventure with their parents to explore
the history, unusual geology, famous sites, plants, and animals
of Olympic National Park. Sidebar notes contain additional
facts about the area and describe the park's regulations and
tourist facilities.
  ISBN 978-1-55591-627-5 (pbk.)
  1. Olympic National Park (Wash.)--Juvenile fiction. [1.
Olympic National Park (Wash.)--Fiction. 2. National parks
and reserves--Fiction. 3. Hiking--Fiction. 4. Vacations--Fiction.
5. Family life--Fiction.] I. Leggitt, Marjorie C., ill. II. Title.
  PZ7.G751574 Tou 2009
  [Fic]--dc22
                                    2008020848

Printed in China

0 9 8 7 6 5 4 3 2 1

Design: Ann W. Douden
Cover image: Marjorie Leggitt
Models for twins: Amanda and Ben Frazier

Fulcrum Publishing
4690 Table Mountain Drive, Suite 100
Golden, CO 80403
800-992-2908 • 303-277-1623
www.fulcrumbooks.com

Morgan, James, Mom, and Dad filed into the
back of the amphitheater. They joined the other visitors at the Heart
O' the Hills campfire program. It was nearly dark and the tall trees were
only silhouettes of their former selves.

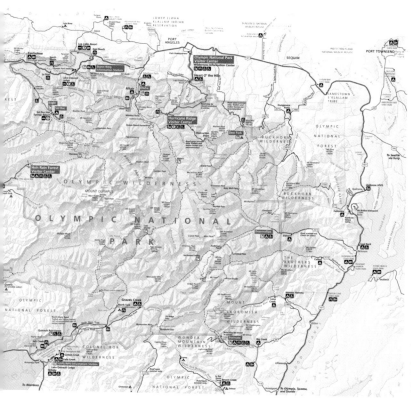

Ten-year-old twins Morgan and James sat on either side of their parents. It was a cool, damp night, and the Parkers huddled close together on the bench and listened to the ranger.

"Now, what do you think the most dangerous animal in the park is?" the ranger asked.

"Mountain lions?" someone called out.

The ranger stalked around the stage, pawed at the air, and let out a growl, then explained. "Mountain lions are potentially dangerous. But," he stressed, "here in Olympic National Park, encounters are extremely rare. With 95 percent of the park protected as wilderness, the mountain lions have abundant terrain and lots of wild food. Any other guesses?"

"Bears?" another visitor asked.

"Ah, the Olympic black bear," the ranger pondered. "Good guess, but in the history of the park, we've never had a black bear attack a human. What else?"

Morgan raised her hand. "Elk?"

"We certainly have elk here," the ranger replied, "but they, too, typically shy away from humans.

"I'll give you a hint," the ranger tantalized the audience. "Think smaller." He buzzed around while spreading imaginary wings.

Just then a family of small, furry animals walked behind the stage.

"Raccoons!" James called out.

The ranger noticed the furry family just as they disappeared into the forest. "They're frequent guests here," the ranger informed the audience, "but think even smaller."

The audience waited for the answer.

"The most dangerous animal in the park builds nests and flies around," the ranger said. "They're responsible for two hundred deaths a year in the United States and thousands of attacks. Furthermore, this tormentor is typically no longer than an average thumbnail."

"Wasps!" somebody exclaimed.

"Exactly!" the ranger replied. "There are twenty different types of wasps in the park, and they all sting. I've been stung a few times myself," he grimaced. "Wasps can sting repeatedly, too. They don't lose their stingers like bees do.

"Once I was taking a shortcut across one of those nurse logs the park is famous for. As I stepped, the wood collapsed and hundreds of wasps swarmed after me."

The ranger yipped and danced around the stage as if he was swatting away a slew of angry wasps. Then he paused, hopped onto an empty bench, and looked at the crowd. "Do you know what I did next? I jumped into the river and swam away." The ranger stepped off the bench. "That's what saved me."

Mom raised her hand. "How many times were you stung?"

The ranger started counting on his fingers. Then he counted them again. "Twenty-four," he announced. "But that's only my best estimate.

"I was lucky," he went on. "I'm not allergic. However, it's a good thing there is treatment for those who are!"

The ranger held up an epinephrine pen, a small cylinder with a needle at the end. "A lifesaver for anyone who is allergic," the ranger announced. "And, in case you aren't sure, keep an eye on the victim for at least twenty minutes. Look for swelling, pain, redness, and, especially, difficulty breathing. If any of these signs occur, immediate medical treatment may be necessary.

"Wasps are dangerous. Even our mule packers constantly look for nests when they haul supplies into the backcountry. A startled pack of mules can be a tricky situation.

"But," the ranger stated dramatically, "don't let wasps stop you from exploring our great park. We have the fastest-growing trees on the planet, over seventy miles of wilderness coastline, incredible rain forests, high mountain glaciers, and some of the cleanest air in the country. So please enjoy Olympic, help keep our park as it is, and come back and visit again."

The audience clapped.

The Parkers stood at the edge of a steep drop-off

on Hurricane Ridge. Meadows of wildflowers covered the hills nearby.
The family gazed down at the deep embankment of snow below them.
Farther up the trail there was a ski lift, but it was closed for the summer.

"I can't believe there's so much snow down there," James said.

"I guess that's why they're practicing ice climbing here," Mom said.

A group of mountaineers with packs was near the bottom of the
snowfield. A woman in a red jacket was standing farther up, instructing
the group.

"If you fall and start sliding," the woman explained, "that's when you perform 'self-arrest.' Roll over onto your stomach and thrust the ice axe into the snow just above your shoulder. Use the weight of your body to push the axe further in. That will act as your brake."

The woman climbed higher up the steep slope. Finally, she made it halfway up the embankment. She noticed the Parkers on the trail above and waved. Morgan and James waved back.

"Okay, here goes," the guide called down to the group. She walked up a few more steps and pretended to slip. The woman slid down the ice, rolled onto her stomach, thrust the axe into the snow and leaned on it, then quickly stopped.

The woman stood up and trudged back down the rest of the way. Her students walked over to their packs, grabbed their ice axes, and climbed the snowfield. They struggled upward and stopped just where the snow was too steep to climb. One by one each person repeated the practice fall and slid down the mountain before braking with their ice axes.

The Parkers watched the mountaineers gather together again at the bottom of the embankment.

"They must be preparing for the high peaks of the park," Mom said.

James turned around and gazed at the series of snow-covered mountains to the west. One peak was taller and bulkier. "Is that Mount Olympus?"

"I bet so," Dad answered. "The park's highest mountain."

OLYMPIC HEIGHTS

On July 4, 1788, Captain John Meares, a British mariner, named Mount Olympus after the home of the Greek gods. On September 22, 1890, the Olympic expedition, led by Lieutenant Joseph P. O'Neil, was the first documented European exploration to make it to the mountain's summit. Several years later, on August 13, 1907, Anna Hubert became the first European woman to climb the mountain.

The family continued their stroll along Hurricane Ridge. "It's pretty unusual to see snow and the ocean from the same trail," Dad commented.

James and Morgan walked ahead to read a small sign next to some purplish flowers perched on thin stalks. "These are called blue bells of Scotland," Morgan said before taking several close-up photos of the petals.

An insect flew up and circled around the Parkers.

Morgan jumped back. "A wasp!" she gasped.

The menacing insect landed on Mom's yellow shirt. Mom swatted at it, then backed away. The wasp took off and eventually landed on a flower.

"Have you ever been stung, Mom?" Morgan inquired.

Mom thought for a moment. "You know, I don't think so."

"So you aren't sure if you're allergic then," James asked.

"I guess I don't know," Mom replied.

James walked up to the next sign. "These are lupine," he announced. James gazed at the thick spread of blue-flowered stalks near the sign. Then he jogged ahead.

At the next plaque, James quickly read the sign, then leaned over a fuzzy, cream-colored flower and smelled it. He sat down on the asphalt trail and took off one of his shoes just as the rest of his family walked up.

James bent his foot to his nose and sniffed his sock.

Morgan looked at James, appalled. "What are you doing?"

James smiled nonchalantly. "Look at the sign."

"American bistort," Morgan read. "The smell of these flowers resembles dirty socks."

Mom looked at James. "Well, what's your prognosis?"

"Here, let me see." Dad knelt down and prepared himself to inhale whatever aroma James's foot produced. He took a whiff of James's clean, white sock. "Hmm. Not enough hiking yet," Dad concluded.

Dad stepped over to a nearby flower and smelled it. "Whew!" he called out. "That does smell like dirty socks!"

"But not mine," James concluded.

"I don't know, we'll have to check later," Dad said.

The family strolled on, passing more flowers and information signs. Morgan noticed several fir trees with dense circular clumps of branches surrounding their bases.

Mom saw where Morgan was looking. "I think," she mused, "that the winds Hurricane Ridge is known for sheer off the upper branches of those trees. Snow covering the bottom branches during the winter protects them from the wind, forming those skirts."

"Interesting," Dad responded.

The Parkers approached an area of reddish pink flowers growing in clumps low to the ground. "Mountain heather!" Mom exclaimed. "I think these are my favorite."

Morgan took several pictures of the flowers just as a person walked up. "Pretty, aren't they?" the hiker commented.

"The wildflowers here are the best I've ever seen," Mom said.

"Have you been to Klahane Ridge?" the woman asked.

"No," Dad replied.

The woman pointed toward a bulging mountain that stood out among others nearby. "That's Klahane Ridge," the woman said. "It's one of my favorite places in the park. And I think it has even better wildflowers than here."

Mom pondered the suggestion "I think you've helped us come up with our plan for tomorrow."

"Glad I could help," the woman said while walking away.

Morgan, James, Mom, and Dad looped back past the ski lift above the snowfield the ice climbers had scaled earlier.

Morgan stared all the way down the embankment. "They're gone," she called out.

James saw two black objects scrambling around far below. "No they're not!" he exclaimed. "They just got back on the snow. And they're climbing really fast!"

The family watched the objects quickly gallop up the snowfield.

"They're bears!" Dad realized.

The bears continued climbing. They reached the steep slope where the mountaineers had stopped. But the bears kept going, moving swiftly up the cliff of snow and ice.

"They make it look so easy," Mom said.

Dad gazed at the approaching animals. "I think," he suggested, "that we ought to move away from here now."

"Good idea," Mom agreed.

Once they were at a safe distance, the Parkers turned around to look.

Both bears had reached the top. One lunged at the other. For a moment the bears wrestled. Then they both let go and briskly slid down the snowfield.

When they reached the bottom, one of the bears got up and chased the other into the forest.

"They're playing, aren't they?" Morgan asked.

"It sure looks like it," Mom answered. "Subadult black bears having fun in the snow and sun."

Morgan, James, Mom, and Dad sat by the shore
of Lake Angeles. They passed around snacks while admiring the beautiful
lake surrounded by craggy peaks.

Not long after, the Parkers packed up and returned to the trail.
They began climbing up a steep, faint path. Soon the trees became sparse
and stunted and the family was in more open, grassy terrain.

Mom stopped to admire the colorful wildflowers. "That woman sure
was right," she commented.

As they continued climbing, the family approached a patch of snow.
James stepped off the trail and scooped through the dirty outer layer of
ice until he found some that was completely white. He gathered up a fresh
handful and packed it together. "It's like having a snow cone," he said.

"Wait a second," Mom called out. "I know it looks clean, but…"

The Parkers heard a clanking sound above them. They turned and
saw two mountain goats walking casually down the same trail they
were going up. The mother goat had fur that was all matted. She also
had a yellow collar around her neck. The other goat, a small kid, followed
its mom.

The two goats strolled along, then turned off the trail and headed
toward James. "What should I do?" James asked.

GOATS ON THE LAM

Mountain goats were introduced into the Olympic park area in the 1920s. They were apparently brought there to be hunted. Many of them settled around Klahane Ridge. The goats thrived in the park, but they also trampled soils, destroyed vegetation, and spoiled habitats. In the 1980s, a removal program started, which included live trapping and sterilization. Trapping didn't always work: several animals were hurt and fled. Also, due to the rugged terrain, there was a risk of trappers getting injured. By the late 1980s, the remaining mountain goats were designated to be shot, but some people protested this as cruel. For now, the decision regarding the park's mountain goats is at a standstill. Goat populations are being monitored, though, and collars have been placed on them to keep track of their numbers. Currently, about 250 to 320 mountain goats live in Olympic National Park.

"Here. Let's give them some room," Dad suggested. He guided his family a few feet down the trail.

The mother goat walked right onto the snow patch, and her kid followed. They made it to the middle of the ice and lay down.

"It's a good thing you didn't eat that," Morgan remarked.

James dropped his snowball, and the family continued climbing on the faint, narrow path. "Sometimes it seems like we're following their trail, not ours," Dad commented.

Eventually, the Parkers approached the top of Klahane Ridge. Once there, they gazed at the ragged, jutting peaks and scattered patches of snow all around them.

Finally, the family made it to the highest point on the trail. They looked west at the massive Olympic mountain skyline and soaked in the scenery for a few more minutes. Then they followed the trail down into a steep mountain bowl covered in small, loose rocks. "Let's take our time here," Mom suggested. "The footing looks pretty precarious."

Dad looked around. "This part of the trail looks almost lunar," he said. "It's so barren."

After trekking carefully down the trail, the family worked their way back up a set of steep switchbacks to another rocky summit.

Mom led the way down the other side of the ridge. She stopped where the trail branched into two paths. "Let's try this way," Mom suggested, stepping carefully down a barely distinguishable trail.

Dad turned around. "Let me check something." He took several steps back up the trail and looked at the other path. "Hmm," he pondered at the junction. "It's hard to tell which way to go."

Dad heard some clanking in the distance and stepped on a rock to get a look. The rock rolled over, and Dad's foot landed in loose soil, which collapsed. Dad slid down the hill in a cascade of small rocks.

"Ahh!" Dad shrieked as he caromed into a boulder and stopped.

Morgan, James, and Mom rushed back up the trail and saw Dad clinging to the steep slope.

"Are you okay?" Morgan shouted.

Dad scrambled to his feet, dislodging more small rocks as he climbed. Finally, Dad returned to the trail. "I'm okay," he reported while brushing himself off. "We better be careful where we step, though."

Lupine.

The Parkers continued traversing the trail. Brilliant carpets of wildflowers blanketed the hillside nearby. The family approached a dilapidated old stone cabin. They passed the ruined shelter and a few minutes later entered the forest. The late afternoon sunlight filtered into the deep woods.

Mom stopped. "Shhh," she whispered.

The Parkers stood still. They could hear a gentle breeze whistling through the trees and the sound of a small stream.

Finally, Morgan spoke. "What?"

The forest answered her. *Hooo. Hoooo.*

"There it is again," Mom said. "An owl."

Hooo. Hoooo.

The family listened to the owl hoot several more times.

"I wonder if it's a spotted owl," Mom mused. "They're endangered and only live in old-growth forests in the Northwest."

"It sounds kind of spooky," James said.

Dad gazed at the darkening forest surrounding them. "Well, evening will be along soon," he said. "And that owl will be off hunting."

"And we'll be eating our own dinner," Morgan added while trotting down the trail toward camp.

After hiking to their car, the family drove out of the park and into the town of Port Angeles. They had a quick dinner there, then drove west, where they re-entered the park along the Elwha River. It was already dark when they pulled into Elwha Campground.

The Parkers found an empty campsite and went to work. Mom and Dad set up the tent while Morgan and James crumpled up pieces of newspaper and dropped them into the fire pit. They put kindling on top, then Dad lit a match to the paper. Soon a small fire was crackling away.

The family set up their chairs close to the fire. "It's chilly out here," Mom said as she passed around a bag of oatmeal cookies.

Dad took a bite out of a cookie. "That Klahane Ridge Trail was about as pretty of a place as I have ever seen!"

"I liked all the wildflowers," Mom added.

After a while, a fine drizzle of rain began to mist down.

Soon drops also fell from the overhanging trees. "I think that's enough for me tonight," Dad announced.

"Me too," Morgan and Mom said in unison. James got up and helped Dad douse what was left of the fire. The family piled into the tent, taking off their wet shoes at the entrance. They slipped into their sleeping bags and listened to the rain's steady beat on the nylon roof.

• • •

The next morning, it was still raining. James rolled over in his sleeping bag and lifted his head to see if anyone else was awake.

Morgan heard James. "I'm up," she said.

"Me too," Mom added.

"Don't forget about me," Dad chimed in.

"What time is it?" Morgan asked.

Dad glanced at his watch. "Wow!" he exclaimed. "9:30."

"We really slept in. I thought it was around 7:00," James replied.

"What do you want to do now?" Morgan asked.

"What do *you* want to do?" Mom replied.

Morgan shrugged her shoulders. "I don't know." Then she slithered deeper into her sleeping bag, reached for her journal, and wrote:

Dear Diary,

It's been raining all night. I guess that's why Olympic is famous for its rain forest. Dad says it rains here almost ten times more than it does at home in California. But I hope we get good weather for the rest of our explorations here.

Yesterday we got lucky. The weather was perfect, and we hiked over twelve miles on the Klahane Ridge Trail. It was an amazing place with great views of the Olympics and the mountains to the east. We even got to share the trail with two mountain goats!

So what about today? Right now Dad's mustering up the courage to step outside. We'll get a weather report from him in a minute.

Trying to keep dry in the rain forest!

Morgan

Dad was now outside, walking around. "It's not that bad," he said. "We'll just have to dress appropriately for the hike."

Mom called out to Dad, "If we wait for the weather here, we might not do that much at all."

A short while later the Parkers were driving on a muddy dirt road.

They parked their car at a trailhead and bundled up in jackets before stepping outside.

The wide pathway wound its way through dense rain forest. The Parkers passed by tall trees, large ferns, and mosses. Morgan, James, Mom, and Dad walked along, squishing with every step. "Sometimes I can't tell if it's still raining or the trees are just dripping," Mom commented.

Soon the family reached a turnoff.

They took the trail to an overlook of the Elwha River where it rushed into a narrow gorge. "Goblins Gate!" Mom exclaimed, recalling a trail guide she'd read.

Morgan studied the rushing river. "The water color looks different."

"It's kind of aqua blue," James said.

"Hmm," Dad pondered while staring at the water.

The Parkers continued trekking along the gently sloping trail. At a junction, the family turned uphill. Soon they passed an old, abandoned cabin.

The Parkers approached another small shack a few minutes later and stepped onto the porch and out of the rain. The family sat down on the worn-out boards.

Mom took off her pack and pulled out a poncho for each of them. "Let's get these on," she urged.

Dad put on the extra rain gear, stood up, and walked up to a sign. "Michael's Cabin," he announced.

Dad continued reading. "I guess they called him Cougar Mike because he was a well-known mountain lion hunter. He also guided people to the top of Mount Olympus."

"I wonder what the weather is like up there now," Morgan pondered.

"Probably a lot worse than here," Mom said while getting up. "I don't think we should wait any longer for the weather to clear."

She stepped out from under the porch and into the gentle rain. The rest of the family followed her. They started hiking back and eventually returned to their car. After they piled in, Dad started the engine and cranked up the heat while they rode back down the muddy road.

The Parkers left the park and passed by Lake Crescent. Soon, Dad turned the car back into Olympic along the Sol Duc River. Near the end of the road, they arrived at a small resort. They checked in, went to their cabin, and quickly got out of their wet clothes and showered. Then the family walked over to the hot springs.

James looked at the three steamy, blue swimming pools full of guests. He dipped his foot into the water of the first pool. "It's hot!" he reported.

And that's where the Parkers spent the rest of the day, in the hot springs at Sol Duc Resort.

The Parkers slept in at their cabin,

then eventually began packing up.

"One night here isn't enough," Mom remarked.

Dad glanced out the window and noticed a gentle, misty rain drifting down. "Especially in this weather," he added.

"But, hey, we are in a rain forest!"

After checking out at 10 AM, the family drove to the end of the road and reached a large parking lot filled with cars. Mom parked near the back, and they piled out with their rain gear on. The Parkers walked to the trail, passing groups of backpackers who were preparing their gear.

"Soon it will be our turn to hike in Olympic's backcountry," Dad said. "Rain or shine, just like them."

The family reached a wide, flat trail and headed out on it. Quickly they were in a dark, wet forest. Several other groups of backpackers also plodded along.

A short while later, the family arrived at a bridge. They could hear the roar of cascades as they approached.

"This must be the falls," James said.

They stopped at the railing and gazed at a set of three waterfalls tumbling into a deep, narrow gorge.

"Beautiful," Mom murmered.

The family stared at Sol Duc Falls for several more minutes.

"It looks so primeval in there," Dad mentioned. "All the plants and ferns make me think of dinosaurs."

"Yeah. It kind of reminds me of *Jurassic Park*," James added.

A ranger walked up. "Hello," he greeted them.

"Hi," Morgan replied.

"Great place, isn't it?" he asked.

"Even in the rain," Dad agreed.

The ranger chuckled. "Oh, you can't let the rain stop you around here."

Dad looked at him. "Do you recommend seeing anything else while we're in the area?"

The ranger thought for a second. "The High Divide Trail, where all the backpackers are going, quickly gets you past the crowds and is a really great place to hike." He smiled. "Also, there are ripe huckleberries not too far off the trail. You are welcome to pick them to snack on. Just remember, the berries also feed the animals."

"It sounds like we just got another great tip!" Mom said.

The Parkers said good-bye to the ranger. They walked past a shelter and took the trail above the falls.

A few minutes later, the family approached a group of scouts spread out among the bushes, eating berries.

"Mind if we join you?" Dad asked.

"There's tons around here," the scout leader replied. "Help yourself!"

Mom looked at a bush next to the trail, then plucked a small, purplish blue berry from it. She wiped it off until it was polished clean. "Okay, here goes."

Mom put the huckleberry in her mouth and bit into it.

Mmm, good!

"Mmmm," she reported. Then Morgan, James, and Dad also indulged.

"This one's really sweet!" Morgan called out.

"Mine's a little sour," James added with a puckered face.

"I'm glad the ranger told us about the berries and we saw these scouts," Dad said. "Otherwise, I wouldn't have known for sure if these were huckleberries."

The Parkers spread out, searching for ripe, juicy berries.

A few minutes later, Dad called to his family, "Had enough yet?"

"I think so," Morgan replied. "We should leave some for the animals."

"Just a couple more," James said while juice trickled down his chin. He reached out and plucked a few more berries and popped them into his mouth. "Mmm, sweet!"

The Parkers headed back toward Sol Duc Falls. There was a wooden shelter nearby. They walked over and peered inside.

A group of backpackers was sitting on camping mattresses spread out on the floor. They huddled together, their backpacks leaning up against a wall.

"They're shivering," Morgan noticed.

Dad took a step closer. "Come on in and join us," one of the backpackers said invitingly.

"Where did you come from?" Dad asked.

"The High Divide," the man replied. "Only we couldn't see a thing up there. It was raining, hailing, and foggy the whole time, until we got near here."

"Are you okay?" Mom asked.

"Yes, we're finally starting to warm up."

"Well, you're not far from the parking lot," Morgan informed the group.

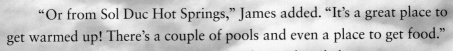

"Or from Sol Duc Hot Springs," James added. "It's a great place to get warmed up! There's a couple of pools and even a place to get food."

The backpackers looked at each other and smiled.

"I forgot about that," one of them said.

The Parkers left the Sol Duc shelter and hiked to their car. Then they took off for the ocean.

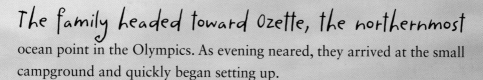

The family headed toward Ozette, the northernmost
ocean point in the Olympics. As evening neared, they arrived at the small
campground and quickly began setting up.

Rays of sunshine slanted across their campsite. "Finally, the weather's
clearing," Mom said.

Morgan noticed a lake nearby. "Look!" she pointed.

Mom glanced over. "A lake right next to the ocean. Pretty neat."

Dad returned from the backcountry permit office down the road.
"Good news," he announced. "The weather is supposed to be dry for the
next few days."

"Perfect timing for our backpack," Morgan replied happily.

• • •

The next morning, after an early breakfast, the family tore down camp,
packed up, and drove over to the nearby trailhead parking lot. They
grabbed their backpacks, slung them over their shoulders, and walked up
to an information sign. Morgan took a picture of her family there before
they headed out.

A moment later they were crossing a bridge over the Ozette River
and entering a thick, dense forest.

The family stepped onto sets of old, rickety wooden planks cutting a path through the trees. "The plants in here are huge!" James exclaimed.

"Yeah, like the leaves on that thing." Morgan pointed.

"That's a skunk cabbage," Mom said. "Go ahead and sniff the leaves, or anywhere on the plant. It smells like a skunk."

Morgan wrinkled her nose. "I think I'll pass."

"Me too," James added.

They walked on silently, hearing only their footsteps on the creaky boards.

Morgan noticed moss on one of the planks and a plant growing through the wood. "An old-growth board!" she joked.

The family continued to trudge along. Eventually, the forest led to a break in the trees. "I can smell the ocean now," Mom announced.

James saw the beach first. "There it is!"

The Parkers gazed through the trees at Olympic's wild, rocky shoreline and the crashing waves in the distance.

"Sound of the ocean," Dad sang, "touch of the sea, always puts my mind at ease."

James looked at Dad. "I didn't know you could sing."

Dad smiled. "I'm not so sure I can."

The family lugged their backpacks through the soft sand and headed toward a harder-packed area near the water.

They headed south, continuing the hike to their campsite.

Morgan gazed at the large, white driftwood logs scattered along the shoreline. "Those trees look like giant dinosaur bones."

Mom stopped and stared into a small pool of tidewater. "Look at these," she called out.

Morgan, James, and Dad hurried over.

"Those shells are moving," Morgan realized.

Mom reached down and picked up one of the little creatures. She placed it in her hand. "Watch."

A moment later a tiny animal partially emerged from its shell. It began to scurry along Mom's palm.

"A hermit crab!" James said.

Mom put the crab back. "Here's a *really* tiny one," Morgan noticed.

"Look at this bigger one," Dad said, pointing.

The family spread out, examining several other tide pools for signs of life.

Dad noticed a large crab with red claws lying motionless on the beach. He gently poked the crab with a small stick, but it didn't move. "It must be dead," he concluded.

James propped up a small rock. A bunch of crabs scurried back under it. "These aren't," he reported. James gently put the rock down.

The Parkers continued their beach trek. The weather was overcast, and waves crashed far from the shore. A bunch of seabirds squawked in the distance.

Dad stopped and took a deep breath. "Ahhh," he exhaled. "It's great to take in some of this clean air."

The family carefully worked their way around a rocky peninsula.

Once on the other side, they hopped from rock to rock, heading back to the beach.

James noticed whale and face drawings etched into a rock. "Who do you think did these?" he asked.

Mom turned to see. "Those look like petroglyphs," she responded. "Ancient drawings from Native Americans."

Morgan took several pictures.

"I wonder how old they are," Dad mused.

Once back on the beach, Dad noticed a large piece of driftwood in an area of soft, dry sand. "Break time!" Dad announced as he strolled over to the log.

The Parkers sat down and leaned back against their makeshift bench. "Anyone else hungry?" Dad asked.

They ate lunch to the sounds of the ocean. Soon the sun poked through the low clouds, warming the beach a few degrees.

Mom put some sunscreen on and passed it to Morgan. She handed it to Dad. Dad coated his arms and face, then gave it to James.

When James was finished, he stuffed the sunscreen into his backpack's side pocket.

Dad yawned and stretched. "How about a little nap?"

While Mom and Dad closed their eyes, Morgan began creating a sculpture in the sand. As she did, James pulled out his journal.

This is James Parker reporting.

My family and I are backpacking on the beach! There are no roads out here, and the only people we've seen are other hikers.

We've been taking our time on the hike. Now there's about one mile left to our campsite.

James looked up and watched Morgan.

Morgan finished creating a series of high mountains with deep valleys below them. Then she arranged a bunch of small twigs beneath the peaks. Next, Morgan traced out a coastline and the ocean. Finally, she sprinkled dry, white sand over the summits of the mountains.

"What are you doing?" James asked.

"I'm making Olympic National Park," Morgan replied. "Here's the rain forest," she said while pointing to the twigs. "And here's the ocean. I was just putting snow on the mountains."

James closed his journal. "Can I help?"

Morgan nodded. James sprinkled more sand over the highest peaks. "That way there'll be enough snow to form a glacier," he explained.

Morgan built one mountain up a little higher. She traced a trail leading toward it. "This is the hike we're going to be on," she said to James.

James grabbed more white sand and Morgan did too. Together they coated several of Olympic's highest peaks in a deep layer of fake snow. Then, suddenly, part of a peak near Mount Olympus collapsed. A pile of dry sand crashed down on a section of Morgan's trail and wiped it out.

"Oops," James said. He grabbed a handful of sand and poured it back on the mountain. But the sand spilled back down the mountain's side, adding to the mini-avalanche.

Morgan and James heard a sound coming from a nearby pile of driftwood. They turned around and looked.

A raccoon crawled out from underneath one of the logs. It wandered around while pawing at objects, searching for food.

James glanced over at Mom and Dad, but they appeared to be asleep.

The raccoon walked closer to the Parkers. Morgan and James watched it scamper onto the same log they were sitting next to. It continued walking toward them.

James looked at Morgan. "Should we wake Mom and Dad?" he whispered.

The raccoon stood on its hind legs, staring at Morgan and James. Then it dropped down and scampered into the forest.

Mom and Dad sat up. "I thought you were asleep," James said.

"I was," Mom answered.

"I like your display of the Olympics," Dad commented.

"You were listening?"

"A bit," Dad replied.

Morgan took a picture of her sand relief map and they trekked on. The family passed a rock formation with a hole in it. James peered through the natural opening and gazed out at the ocean. "It's a little window," he said.

Soon they walked into the tidal zone toward another jutting peninsula of rock.

"I think it's almost high tide now," Mom commented, noticing the water level.

Mom led the way past pools of seawater. She hopped onto a rock and turned to extend her hand out to James. "Careful, it's slippery out here," she warned.

The family climbed across the rocky, wet terrain, staying close to the bluff that rose above them.

James noticed a starfish hugging one of the rocks in the water. "Look, over there," he said, pointing.

The family gazed into the tide pool, but a wave crashed nearby, churning up the water and obstructing the view. Mom took a step back against the bluff. "Come over here," she guided her family.

The Parkers watched what was left of the wave fill in the pools all around them. Finally, the foamy water stopped surging forward, just below their feet.

"There isn't any more room for us," Dad realized, staying close to the cliff. Dad looked back toward shore, trying to pick out a safe path to return on.

James noticed a larger wave breaking farther out. It pummeled the rocks, sending a spray of water high into the air. The wave filtered in toward the Parkers. They pressed themselves up against the rock wall, preparing for an onslaught of water. But the wave died off several yards away.

Mom looked at the ocean and saw another wave forming. Then she glanced back toward the beach and saw a red-and-black sign posted on a tree.

The large wave poured into the tidal zone.

"Get back!" Mom yelled.

The Parkers pressed against the cliff. The wave rolled in and crashed on a rock nearby, sending a spray of foamy water over the family.

Morgan, James, Mom, and Dad held on as water showered over them. Then the wave slowly returned to sea.

"That was way too dangerous," Mom said. She looked back at the sign. "Quick, follow me," she called out.

The family retreated back through the seaweed-covered rocks and finally returned to the beach.

"That sign must mark the place to pass safely during high water," Mom stated while walking toward the tree. "Yep, there's a rope up there for us to climb."

"There has to be a safer way to continue our hike," Dad said.

Mom grabbed the rope and started scrambling up a worn trail, passing tree trunks and roots along the way. She reached a second, thicker rope and paused to look down at her family.

James climbed next. He pulled himself up toward Mom. "It's like being on an obstacle course in my PE class!" James exclaimed.

As Morgan joined James, Mom continued climbing. Dad went last. Eventually, they were all perched at the top of the bluff.

The Parkers gazed down at the ocean waves crashing onto the shore. "Pretty cool view up here, huh?" Dad said.

Mom took a few steps and looked over the other side. "What goes up must go down," she announced.

Mom grabbed the rope on that side of the bluff. She stepped down backward, carefully placing her feet on the loose dirt along the way.

When she got to the bottom, she watched a small trickle of rocks careen down the hill. As soon as the rocks had stopped, Mom called out, "Okay, all clear." Once back on the beach, the family continued trekking south.

"That was fun!" James exclaimed.

A bunch of barking sounds came from the surf. Morgan gazed out at a series of rocks. "Something on one of the rocks just moved," she called out.

Mom stopped and looked. "I think those are seals!"

"We're getting to see a little bit of everything today," Dad said.

James noticed an old buoy hanging from a tree. Several tents were nearby. "Look up there," he pointed.

The family clambered toward the forested campsite. "It's first come, first served out here," Dad said, looking around. They found an empty area, quickly set up their tent, and began gathering food together. James noticed the sun approaching the horizon. "Sunset!" he announced.

"That looks like a great place to see it from," Mom said, pointing to a small bluff.

Dad glanced up from cooking. "Why don't the three of you head up there while I finish making dinner?"

Morgan, James, and Mom climbed the trail up the small hill. They stood there admiring the views and the orange sky along the horizon.

Two glistening, sleek gray bodies broke through the surface of the water.

"Look!" James called out.

They watched the ocean animals glide along before disappearing beneath a curling wave. Then the animals resurfaced several yards farther out. "Dolphins," Mom gasped.

Morgan looked back at camp and saw Dad using the binoculars to watch the dolphins too.

The Parkers watched for a few more minutes. Then James, Morgan, and Mom hiked back to join Dad for dinner.

After dinner, the fog blew back in.

The Parkers hung all their food on the bear wires. Then the damp air chased the family into the tent.

Dad slithered into his sleeping bag and zipped it up. "Something about cool, foggy weather and the sound of the waves, and I sleep like a baby," he announced.

Sometime in the middle of the night, James opened his eyes. He strained to listen to scratching sounds outside. Then something crashed to the ground. James grabbed his flashlight.

Morgan was now awake too. "What do you think it is?" she whispered anxiously.

"I don't know," James replied. He slowly unzipped the tent window until it was partially open. James shone his light around. He saw his backpack lying facedown on the ground.

James turned to Morgan. "My pack fell," he reported.

The scratching sounds returned. James looked outside again. He caught a glimpse of a pair of eyes reflecting back the light.

A furry, striped animal climbed on top of James's backpack. It started pawing away at one of the pockets.

"It's a raccoon," James said to Morgan. "And it's trying to get into my pack."

Dad quickly sat up. "Where?"

"Right outside," James replied.

James checked again. This time there were four raccoons, two large ones and two kits, or baby raccoons.

James heard something tear. He saw the raccoons shredding the pocket. "The sunscreen!" James called out.

Dad grabbed a flashlight and opened up the tent door. He crawled outside and stood up. "Get out of here!" he called to the raccoon family. "Go!"

The largest raccoon stood up on its hind legs, facing Dad. Dad bluff-charged the four animals. "Get out of here," he roared again.

The raccoon hissed at Dad before dropping down on all fours and leading its family toward the forest. The animals stopped and looked back once more. Dad ran at them again, and they disappeared into the bushes.

Dad walked over to James's pack. He propped it up against the tree and inspected it. "It's near the bottom," James called from the tent.

Dad found the bottom pocket all torn up and covered with sunscreen. He reached inside and pulled out the shredded container, getting lotion all over his hand.

James watched Dad. "Sorry," he said sheepishly. "I forgot I put it in there."

Dad walked over to the bear wires and started lowering their food bags. Meanwhile, James hurried out of the tent and grabbed several paper

towels. He cleaned up the sunscreen as best as he could, then joined Dad. Together they stuffed sunscreen and gooey paper towels into their garbage.

Dad and James tied the bags, including the garbage, and hauled everything back up.

"Now I know these wires are also for the raccoons," Dad said.

"And I know not to leave anything with a scent in my pack," James added.

Dad and James returned to the tent, and the Parkers went back to sleep.

• • •

In the morning, James peered out of the tent window. *My pack's still standing. Good*, he thought to himself.

James crawled outside and inspected his pack in the daylight. The bottom pocket was torn, but that was all. *I'll still be able to use it*, he concluded.

He walked over and sat on a nearby log, gazing out over the ocean. A misty fog hovered over the beach as seabirds squawked and flew around. *The waves seem so calm now*, James observed.

Dad came out of the tent and joined James. "Do you want to go for a walk?" Dad asked.

"Sure," James replied, and he and Dad took off down the beach.

When they reached the hard sand near the shore, Dad stopped James. "Look at these," he said, pointing.

They stared at a set of large, fresh paw prints embedded in the sand. "What do you think they're from?" James asked.

Dad looked closer. "Definitely not a raccoon," he replied.

James peered into the forest and saw a large black animal. "Over there," he whispered.

A bear was pawing a downed tree. It rolled the log over, inspecting the ground underneath it.

Dad glanced at the sand leading to the bear. "These must be its tracks," he pointed out.

They watched the bear for a few minutes. It lifted the log and sniffed at the ground. Soon the bear wandered back into the forest. Then Dad and James headed back toward camp.

• • •

When Dad and James returned, Morgan and Mom were getting breakfast ready.

"You'll never guess what we saw!" James blurted out.

"Another raccoon?" Morgan guessed.

"Nope," James replied.

"More dolphins?" Mom tried.

Finally James told them. "A bear!"

"Really?" Mom asked. "A bear on the beach. How close was it?"

"It was about a hundred feet away," James replied. "Right, Dad?"

"Maybe a bit more," Dad said.

The Parkers ate their breakfast. They leisurely packed their belongings and begrudgingly began walking the three miles back to Ozette.

"It's hard to say good-bye to the ocean," Mom reflected along the way.

When the family got to their car, they loaded up their packs and began a long drive to the Hoh Rain Forest. They stopped in the small town of Forks along the way to get supplies.

• • •

It was midafternoon by the time they headed back into the main part of the park, inland from the ocean. Just past the entrance station, Mom saw several cars along the side of the road. She slowed down and noticed people with cameras.

"Here, let me pull over," she said.

Mom parked the car and the Parkers piled out. They walked toward the group of people.

James saw a herd of animals basking on a sandbar next to the river. "It's a bunch of elk!" he exclaimed.

"Roosevelt elk," Dad added. "They're darker in color than the ones that live in the Rockies."

The elk were all clumped together in one area. Several of the animals flicked their ears and twitched their legs and tails, chasing away a persistent swath of pestering bugs.

"They're sunbathing," Morgan suddenly realized.

The family watched the elk for several more minutes. Then they drove to the campground and found an empty site. Afterward, they hurried to the visitor center and joined a guided ranger walk on the Hall of Mosses Trail.

PRIZE ELK

Olympic was originally designated a national monument in 1909 by Teddy Roosevelt using the Antiquities Act, which is a government act that sets land aside for preservation. The main reason was to preserve the elk. At that time, elk were being hunted for their teeth, which were prize possessions often worn on belts. Because of that, the elk population had dwindled to around four hundred.

When Olympic became a national park in 1938, it was almost called Elk National Park. Now, because they are protected, about five thousand Roosevelt elk live in Olympic National Park. It is the largest wild population of this type of elk in the world.

A ranger stopped in front of a small, clear creek.

"Thank you for joining me on this hike. My name is Jordan. And this is my favorite little trail in the park," he announced. "And speaking of little, do you see anything moving around in the water?"

Morgan was next to the stream. "Baby fish!" she called out.

"Right you are, young lady," Jordan responded. "The hatchlings here are very special. They're the only fish in the world that are born in freshwater but live most of their lives in the ocean."

"Salmon?" someone from the group asked.

"Yep, salmon," Jordan replied. "These salmon will grow up and swim all the way to Asia over the next three years. Then they have to come right back here, where they were born, in order to spawn. Of the four hundred or so hatchlings, only three or four make it back. Old-growth forests with clear, fresh streams like this one are the perfect habitat for their survival."

The group followed Jordan up a small hill. He stopped in front of a large tree and leaned against the trunk while he waited for everyone to gather around. "This is one of the special inhabitants of our rain forest. It's a three-hundred-foot-tall Douglas fir." Jordan patted the trunk. "That's as long as a football field."

"Temperate rain forests are very rare," he explained. "First, they need old-growth trees. That means the area has never been logged. There also must be nurse logs, and the forest must get over one hundred inches of rain a year."

Jordan looked at the group. "Besides here in northwest Washington, does anyone know where else this type of rain forest occurs?"

Mom spoke up. "In parts of northern California?"

"Correct," Jordan replied.

"New Zealand and Australia?" another person asked.

"Yes, in a few places along the coast there," Jordan stated.

Then the group was quiet.

"And," the ranger finished, "parts of the Alaskan coastline. That's about all the places there are."

Jordan began walking. He stopped near a giant downed tree with a row of small trees growing out of it.

"There's one of our famous nurse logs," he said as he pointed to the flattened tree. "But standing next to it is what we like to call the 'rock star of the forest.'"

Jordan looked at the group. "It's a giant Sitka spruce. Those puppies are our most massive trees, and they are the fastest-growing things on Earth. We measured one that grew over sixty cubic feet in one season!

"You can tell a Sitka spruce by its potato-chip-shaped, puzzlelike sections of bark," the ranger continued. He gazed at the giant tree with admiration.

"Just like some rock stars, though, their grandeur doesn't last long. That nurse log is also a Sitka spruce. But since they only send their roots down less than five feet, many of them topple over during winter storms. Because of that, they usually don't live longer than three hundred years. However, that nurse log will now provide three hundred years of nutrients for the trees growing on it, acting like a time-release vitamin. We call the row of new trees a colonnade, and eventually they'll dissolve what is left of the log."

Jordan guided the group into a deep, shady area with trees that were gnarled and covered in moss.

"Welcome to the famous Hall of Mosses," the ranger announced while gazing up at the Gothic-cathedral-like, dark forest. "These trees are bigleaf maples. They get the most moss on them because more water stays on their bulky trunk and branches."

James leaned toward Morgan. "It looks like the trees have giant beards."

Jordan heard James. "Yep. We call the moss *beards* too. But you should see this place during the winter rains. With all the water they soak up, the mosses swell to ten times their current size. These mosses are also an excellent example of another type of plant Olympic is famous for: epiphytes."

"Ep-i-phytes," Morgan whispered to remember the pronunciation.

"Epiphytes are plants that grow on other plants, and you can see them throughout the Olympic rain forest," the ranger explained.

After answering a few questions, Jordan concluded the talk. "So, thank you for coming and please enjoy your stay in the park. The visitor center is straight ahead on the trail."

The group clapped, then Jordan trotted off.

Morgan, James, Mom, and Dad hung out in the Hall of Mosses for a few more minutes. Morgan took several pictures of the giant, twisted trees and their dangling beards.

Afterward, they walked to the visitor center and stopped at the backcountry desk for their wilderness permit. ·

• • •

"Ah, yes, Blue Glacier, one of the most spectacular sights you'll ever see!" the backcountry ranger exclaimed. "And where did you want to camp?"

Mom began telling the ranger their itinerary but was interrupted by the phone ringing.

"Hang on a second," the ranger said to Mom. "This call might affect your plans.

"Hello…Okay, yes, I understand…But people are getting through?… Great. Thanks."

The ranger hung up the phone. Dad looked at him, concerned. "What's going on?"

"There was a slide yesterday in an avalanche chute on the way to the glacier," the ranger answered. "It wiped out a whole section of trail, but

luckily, no one was hurt."

Morgan and James looked at each other, remembering the collapsing mountain on their sand map.

"We can get through though, right?" Mom asked for reassurance.

The ranger thought for a moment. "That was the backcountry ranger on the phone. He is monitoring the situation, and several hiking groups have already made it by. Once you get up there, you'll have to make the decision whether to cross yourselves—that is, unless another rockfall destabilizes it further."

"Where is it?" Dad asked.

"Just below Glacier Meadows, the last campsite before the spur trails to the glacier."

The Parkers finished getting their permit, then walked out on the Spruce Nature Trail.

At the end of the short path, the family approached a clearing and gazed out at the sandbar leading to the Hoh River. Morgan noticed footprints in the sand. "Can we go out there?"

"Sure," Mom responded.

The family scampered onto the sand and followed the tracks until they got to the river.

James stared into the rushing, milk-colored water. "It's whitish blue," he said.

Dad peered up at the forested mountains surrounding the river valley. "Hmm," he pondered. "The glaciers up there must be grinding rock flour into the ice. That's what's making it this weird color."

James got an idea. "It's pretty warm out right now," he thought out loud. "And there are glaciers above us made of ice and snow, so…"

James looked at his family then back at the water. "I wonder if the water level is higher than it was this morning because the afternoon sun is melting the snow."

"Interesting thinking," Mom responded.

James found a small stick and walked up to the edge of the rapidly flowing water. He pushed the stick into wet mud so it was poking out of the river near a rock.

"There's our marker," James announced. "Can we come back here in the morning and see if the water level lowered overnight, when the temperature cooled down?"

"Of course," Mom said.

Morgan took a picture of the stick poking out of the river. "Our little science experiment," she added.

Mom put her arms around the twins and turned them toward camp. "Come on. We better get some brain food into your inquisitive minds."

James rolled out of his sleeping bag first thing in the morning. Morgan heard him. "Do you want to go check the stick now?" she asked.

James nodded.

Mom slowly opened her eyes. "I'll go with you two."

They got dressed and walked to the end of the Spruce Nature Trail. James hustled to the river first.

It was a clear morning, and the Olympic Mountains surrounded them. The river's bluish white, milk-colored waters rushed by.

The stick was still there. James, Morgan, and Mom looked at it, the rock, and the shoreline.

"It *might* be a little higher out of the water," James said uncertainly.

"Here, let me do this," Morgan suggested. She took another photo from the same spot as the day before. Then, with Mom and James looking over her shoulder, Morgan flipped the pictures back and forth on her digital camera.

"It's really hard to tell if the water level is lower," Morgan said.

"I agree," Mom said.

Morgan, James, and Mom headed back to camp. Dad was cooking breakfast when they arrived. James reported the news on their experiment.

"We'll have to check again when we're done backpacking," Dad suggested.

After breakfast, the Parkers packed up camp and got their packs ready for their three-day journey to Blue Glacier. They drove over to the nearby overnight parking lot. The family piled out of the car and began the long trek.

The Parkers hiked along a shady, mostly flat trail paralleling the Hoh River. They passed the first backcountry campsite at the .9-mile marker.

The family kept walking through the rain forest. Morgan noticed a row of trees growing out of a decaying log. "A colonnade," she recalled.

"That's right. And does anyone remember what kind of tree that is?" Mom pointed.

"Hello, rock star!" James said to the tree.

"You got it," Mom said. "A Sitka spruce."

The Parkers walked on, passing a waterfall at mile marker 2.3. Eventually they approached the signpost labeled Five Mile Island. Dad found a log to sit on and took off his pack. "How about some lunch here?" he suggested.

Morgan, James, and Mom also shed their packs and joined Dad.

James saw an animal dash out from behind some bushes and chase after a squirrel. "A coyote!" he called out.

The squirrel scampered up a tree. The coyote ran to the base of the tree and watched the squirrel while hopping back and forth frantically. Then it saw the Parkers. It stopped and stared at them.

Morgan slowly reached for her camera, but the coyote bounded off and was soon out of sight.

"I love the wilderness!" Mom exclaimed.

After lunch the Parkers hiked on, passing more campsites along the way.

By late afternoon, they rolled into Olympus Guard Station. It had a ranger cabin, a shelter, bear wires, a privy, and people wandering about.

"It's like a little village in here," Mom commented.

The Parkers stopped to use the privy. While they were waiting, James pointed to a sign.

"Bear Frequenting Area," he read.

"We'll have to keep our eyes out," Mom said. "But it's nice to know Olympic has never had a bear hurt a person."

The family continued on. The late-afternoon August sun filtered through the trees lining the trail. "I feel a touch of fall in the air," Dad stated.

"Me too," Mom agreed. "Soon enough the rainy season, which up here is late September through May, will return and this whole forest will be bombarded with storms."

"And the water cycle will continue," Dad added.

Finally they arrived at Lewis Meadow. They left the main trail and found a flat, grassy site next to a tree. "Now this is a great place to camp," Dad said, referring to the open field.

After setting up their tent, Morgan, James, Mom, and Dad followed a faint path to the Hoh River. They walked across an area covered by sand and rocks and approached the rushing water.

"The river's even more weird-looking here," Mom said.

"It reminds me of what *hoh* means," Dad said. "Milky white."

"This river sure fits that description," Morgan added.

James took the filter and found a pool of clearer water to work with. "How about I turn this into some fresh, thirst-quenching glacial water?" he called out.

"You sound like a commercial," Morgan replied.

A few minutes later, they each took a sip of the icy water. "It sure tastes good, James," Dad said.

They trudged back to camp and cooked dinner. After cleaning up, the family piled into their tent and sleeping bags early, hoping for extra energy for tomorrow.

The next morning, the family got up just after sunrise. It was cool out, and misty sunlight filtered through the trees. After the family ate breakfast, they packed up.

"I feel like a kid on Christmas morning," Dad said. "I've wanted to hike to Blue Glacier for a long time."

"Why didn't you go before now?" Morgan asked.

"Some friends and I tried, years ago, when I was in college. But it rained the whole time, and we never made it."

After Lewis Meadow, the trail finally began to climb. Dad kept thinking about the glacier ahead. "Olympic is the only place in the United States, outside of some coastal sections of Alaska, where you can hike from the rain forest to a glacier on the same trail," he commented.

Soon they approached a bridge. Two backpackers were walking across it. "How is it up there?" Mom inquired.

The hikers stopped. One replied enthusiastically, "You definitely have some serious climbing ahead, but it's worth every step of the way."

"Did you get through that slide area okay?" Dad asked.

"It's quite dicey there," the hiker replied. "But you can see where people have been going across. We followed the path and got through without a problem."

The Parkers stepped up to the bridge's railing. They gazed into two deep gorges with rushing streams. "Wow!" Dad exclaimed. "Now that water is just bizarre looking."

"It looks like liquid metal," James added. "It's so gray."

A glacier's movement creates a fine rock called glacial flour. These particles of rock, silt, or clay are caused by the glacier scraping over rock in its path. The flour then flows out from beneath the glacier, in the meltwater. Glacial flour in rivers and lakes often gives off an aqua blue, white, or grayish color. Sometimes this rock flour and water mixture is called glacial milk.

The family soon crossed another log cut to make a small footbridge. A while later, they approached Elk Lake. Several tents were set up nearby.

The Parkers found an empty, flat area to camp. They ate a quick snack, clipped all their extra food into the bear wires, and hoisted the gear high up. Then they took off for Blue Glacier with just their daypacks.

After climbing for several minutes, the family came to a clearing. Far across the way was a large river of ice dropping into a canyon. Dad pulled out his binoculars and studied it. "Now that's a glacier!" he exclaimed.

"I can hear water pouring out of it all the way from here," James said. Then he pulled out his map.

"What glacier is it?" Dad asked.

James showed the map to Dad and Morgan. "I think it's this one, White Glacier."

"What makes that a glacier and not just a bunch of snow?" Morgan asked.

"Good question!" Dad responded. "Glaciers never completely melt. They also are at least one hundred feet deep. And," Dad added, "they typically have cracks with blue ice in them, from their movement."

BLUE ICE

When sunlight passes through solid ice crystals in a glacier, the light gets broken or fragmented into the many colors of the rainbow. The reds and yellows get absorbed by the thick ice. Blue light has more energy, though, and is able to shine through the solid ice crystals. Glaciers have ice that is so dense they absorb all the colors in the spectrum except blue.

Mom hiked on and the family followed. They turned a bend in the trail, and Mom quickly held her arms out, signaling for the family to stay back. A mountain goat was lying on the trail in front of them, flicking its ears back and forth.

Mom slowly approached, but the goat didn't budge.

"Look at how white its fur is," Morgan commented.

"Maybe it's one of the Three Billy Goats Gruff," James joked.

"It looks almost tame," Dad added.

Soon the Parkers were within a few feet of the goat. "It isn't moving," Mom reported, "but I don't really see an easy way around it."

Morgan took several close-up pictures. "It's just sitting there, like it's posing for the camera."

Mom spontaneously clapped her hands several times. The goat rose up and scrambled several feet above the trail.

James kept his eye on the goat as he and his family scampered past it. "I feel like I'm on one of those animal shows on TV," he said.

Mom led the way up and around another bend. She turned the corner and stopped again.

"Here's the slide," Mom called back. She examined the section of trail that was wiped out and the faint, newly created path through it. "And there's where people have been crossing it."

The path cut right through the steep chute, passing by several exposed roots of toppled trees. The Parkers could hear small trickles of rocks slipping down.

Mom examined the makeshift trail. "Let me give this first part a try," she said, then swallowed nervously.

Mom gingerly stepped into the slide area and carefully walked along the narrow, exposed path. She stopped at a stable point and turned back. "Just take your time and step slowly," she coached. "I'll wait for all of you here."

One by one, Morgan, James, and Dad hiked up to Mom. They tightroped their way over loose rocks, and soon they gathered together again and surveyed the next section.

"So far, so good," Mom reported.

"Except we're out in the middle of the avalanche area," James said while thinking of Morgan's sand map.

Mom took a step into the second wiped-out section. A small cascade of rock debris spilled down the chute. She stepped back. "I guess the trick is to move quickly," Mom instructed, "but watch where you put your feet."

The family cautiously worked their way across the second section. *I feel like I'm walking on a balance beam in gym class,* Morgan thought, *Only this one is full of loose rocks and isn't level.*

The family regathered for the last section of the chute and trekked quickly across it. Finally, they had made it back to the real trail.

"Well, that's done for now," Mom announced, thinking of the return trip.

The Parkers hiked on, passing Glacier Meadows campsite.

They stopped at a warning sign posted before the final ascent to the glacier. Dad read it silently and summarized the message for his family: "Hidden crevasses, weak snow bridges, and snowstorms can trap people on the mountain, making travel difficult or impossible. There can also be white-out conditions." Dad turned to his family. "But we're not actually going out onto the glacier," he said for reassurance.

Mom took a deep breath. "So, what are we waiting for?"

Morgan, James, Mom, and Dad hiked on.

The trail steepened, and their pace slowed down. Trees around the area became more stunted and sparse.

Dad glanced up at the boulder field the trail climbed through. "We're so high up, it feels like we're on a gondola," he said.

The Parkers gathered together next to a large patch of snow. Mom walked across it, following the footprints of previous hikers. She flattened each step in the slushy snow, creating more traction for the rest of her family.

Once past the snow, the family kept a slow, steady pace while stepping up and over small boulders.

Finally, the trail started to level off. As it did, the Parkers got their first glimpse of the arctic-like scene ahead. "Look at those chunks of ice on the mountain," James said of the slopes to their left.

After a few more steps, the Parkers made it to the top of the ridge.

From there, they got a close-up view of Mount Olympus and its glacier-clad summit. Just below the mountain, Blue Glacier stretched out across a long, wide valley.

"Wow!" Dad gasped. "That is one massive glacier." He stared at the several-mile-long sheet of ice. "It's more spectacular than I ever imagined." Then Dad gazed at the high peaks and mountains covered in snow. "I wonder how many other glaciers are visible from here."

"Look at all the blue cracks in the glacier!" Morgan exclaimed while gazing down. "I can see where it gets its name now."

"I feel like we're in Patagonia or Alaska somewhere," Mom added.

Morgan fumbled through her daypack. She pulled out her camera and directed everyone to stand on the ridge so that Mount Olympus and Blue Glacier were in the background. Then Morgan set her camera on a rock and adjusted it so that it was level. She pushed down on the automatic timer button and ran over to join her family.

"That will be the first of many pictures up here," Morgan announced after the camera clicked.

Dad wrapped his arms around his family. "We're at the destination of a lifetime!" he exclaimed.

The Parkers sat down and passed around snacks while continuing to gaze at the scenery.

"I wonder how thick that ice is," James mused while staring at a huge crevasse. The large crack started at the surface of the glacier and turned a vivid blue near the bottom.

Several popping and churning sounds came from the glacier. "Wow, listen to that," Morgan said.

"It's like a giant, slow-motion conveyor belt down there," Dad explained. "Those noises are caused by the glacier moving."

Then James pulled out his journal.

This is James Parker reporting.

I'm sitting here on a thin slab of rocks called a moraine. Dad says moraines are piles of rocks moved by a glacier. And we sure have a huge glacier below us. What I am looking at is something I have only seen in pictures. It's kind of like being back in the Ice Age, or on Shackleton's voyage to the Antarctic.

And the glacier is making noises! We've now heard it crack, creak, and roll rocks around. Also, we can hear water moving somewhere in the glacier, but we can't see it.

Dad says this trail is something we'll remember forever. Mom calls it a "glamour trail." That means very few people get here, but those that do show off their pictures and tell stories for the rest of their lives.

Anyway, I wish I could put all that I'm seeing into words. But as the saying goes, "I guess you had to be there." I'm glad I'm here, that's for sure.

Reporting from Blue Glacier,

James Parker

Morgan elbowed James. "There are people moving near the top of the mountain. I've been watching them for a few minutes."

James put away his journal and looked. "They're so small," he said.

Mom pulled out the binoculars. She followed the mountaineers for a moment. "They're climbing down," she realized.

The family passed the binoculars around as they watched the climbers descend the steep part of the glacier.

Dad took a long look. "They're roped together," he reported while passing the binoculars to James.

James found the climbers. "The person in back has a red jacket on."

Morgan followed the six mountaineers as they slowly traversed the upper part of Blue Glacier. "It doesn't look like there are as many crevasses up there," she said. "It's probably a safer place to cross."

Mom gazed at the summit of Mount Olympus and noticed wisps of snow and ice being blown off the peak. Then she looked at the climbers. The first group was nearly across the ice, approaching the rock field to the side of the glacier. The last three climbers were about a hundred feet behind them.

Mom looked back at the summit of the mountain. But it was now buried in clouds.

The breeze picked up. "I'm getting cold," Morgan said.

"Me too," James agreed. "Probably because of that giant freezer of ice below us."

James put on his yellow jacket.

Dad studied the sky. Bands of clouds were now being blown across the peaks, obscuring their view. "I think a storm is brewing," he announced.

The Parkers glanced back at the climbers. The first group was completely off the ice while the other three were still scrambling across on the snow.

James watched them for a moment. "Something happened," he exclaimed. "One of the climbers disappeared. And the other two are lying in the snow with their ice axes planted. It looks like they're doing self-arrest!"

"Can I see?" Morgan asked.

Morgan took the binoculars and looked at the three climbers on Blue Glacier. "Someone from the group off the snow is running back out there."

Morgan watched for another minute. "I think one of the climbers fell into a crevasse and they're trying to get him out."

The wind kicked up again. Dad scanned the horizon. Mount Olympus and the surrounding peaks were now completely enshrouded in clouds. "I think," Dad concluded, "that we should consider heading down now."

The Parkers packed up their snacks. Morgan took one more glance at the glacier with the binoculars but couldn't see the climbers. "It's all fogged in now," she reported.

The family reluctantly began their trek back.

Mom again led the way.

They walked down through the boulder field, and Mom skated across the snow patch. "It's kind of fun that way," she commented. James, Morgan, and Dad copied her.

Soon the trail approached the more forested area and became less rocky. The Parkers reached the side trail to the glacier's terminal moraine.

PARTS OF A GLACIER

- **Bergschrund:** A crevasse near the top of a glacier, formed where ice is thick enough to move or break away from nonmoving ice.
- **Coulier:** A steep gully of ice that goes from a glacier up to a ridge.
- **Crevasse:** Open cracks in glacial ice.
- **Moraine:** Rock debris deposited by a glacier. Lateral moraines are along the glacier's sides. Terminal moraines are at the end of the glacier.

Dad glanced at the cloudy skies and then at his family. "Should we check it out?" he asked. "When's the next time we're going to be this close to Blue Glacier?"

The Parkers began walking on the half-mile spur trail. They climbed up to a rocky point overlooking the end of the glacier. Right below them was the glacier's tongue, dipping down between some rocks.

"We're really close to some blue cracks now," James observed.

Morgan took pictures. Then the glacier made a funny sound.

James laughed. "I think the glacier just burped!"

After a few more minutes staring at the end of the glacier, the family hiked back.

As soon as they reached the main trail, they continued down, heading to their campsite at Elk Lake.

A few minutes later, the family approached the giant slide. They all stared at the precarious-looking pathway.

"Well, we crossed it on the way up, we should be able to again," Mom said, trying to reassure everyone. She gently took the first step into the chute. A few tiny rocks dislodged and tumbled down. Mom turned and looked at her family. "Let's stay a few feet apart," she directed, "so we're not all putting our weight on the same exact spot."

One by one, the family carefully stepped into the avalanche area. When they reached the end of the first of the three sections, Mom waited. "Is everyone okay?" she asked.

Morgan and James nodded. "So far, so good," Dad responded from the back.

Mom surveyed the next section. "This part is the most treacherous, I think." She took a step onto it.

Slowly the Parkers worked their way across the next part of the slide. Morgan glanced down at the steep chute full of loose rocks and grabbed a small root sticking out of the cliff, for balance.

A mini-cascade of pebbles dislodged near the root and showered down. Morgan quickly let go of the plant and scurried past it. Mom turned and reached out toward Morgan. She grabbed Morgan's arm and held her on the path. "You can't really tell what's stable in here at all," Mom said comfortingly.

James came up to where Morgan had been. He peered down at the rocks now settling near the bottom of the chute.

"Keep moving," Dad called. "This is not exactly a place to hang out."

James took Dad's direction and scampered past the roots. The family gathered again before the last section.

Morgan turned to James. "Sorry about that."

"It's okay," James replied. "I would have grabbed the root too, until I saw what happened to you."

"One last section," Mom encouraged. "Are you all ready?"

"Yes," the rest of the family replied.

Mom stepped up the small hill that marked the beginning of the last part of the slide. She made it to the highest part, then turned around. "There's a decent path in here," she called back. "But," Mom glanced at the downhill section of the trail, "the rocks in this area look quite loose, so be careful."

Mom quickly stepped down the last part of the slide. She reached the main trail, then turned back to watch Morgan, James, and Dad.

"You're doing great!" Mom said, cheering them on.

Morgan attempted to smile, but her nerves prevented it. She stepped up to the top of the section, then gazed down at the rest.

James caught up to Morgan. He took a step, then realized in midair that Morgan wasn't moving. James pulled his foot back, and it landed awkwardly below the narrow trail.

An area of loose rocks caved in, sending a plume of debris down the chute. James yanked his foot up and stepped back onto the path just as Dad caught up.

The three of them stood briefly on the trail's high point.

"I'm just going," Morgan suddenly called out. She quickly whisked down the last section and made it to Mom.

James and Dad followed Morgan's lead.

A moment later they were all together again on the safety of the real trail. "Whew!" Dad said with relief.

The family gazed out at the avalanche area they had just come through, inspecting the difficulty of what they had accomplished.

Mom put her arms around Morgan and James.

"That took a lot of courage. Nice job!" she praised.

An insect buzzed around the Parkers. Mom saw it head toward Morgan. She swatted at it, but it flew toward Morgan again. "A wasp!" Mom exclaimed.

The wasp circled the Parkers several more times before heading for James's bright yellow jacket. The wasp landed on his arm, and he hastily shook it off.

Then the menacing insect buzzed toward Mom. She instinctively took a step back and lifted her arm to swat at it.

The wasp flew right at Mom's face, landing on her cheek. "Ah!" Mom hollered while stepping back again.

The ground beneath Mom's foot collapsed as she shifted her weight onto a slew of loose rocks. She instantly slid down, pummeled by debris along the way.

Morgan, James, and Dad stood frozen in horror as they watched Mom roll down the avalanche chute.

"Mom!" James screamed while he and Morgan took a step forward.

Dad grabbed them. "Wait," he warned, "you can't go down there."

Finally, Mom stopped about fifty feet below the trail. She lay motionless, with her head facing the ground.

"Kristen!" Dad hollered.

"Mom!" Morgan called out.

After several tense seconds, Mom finally moved one of her legs. Then she lifted her head and groaned.

She tried to shift her weight, but the debris gave way and she slid a few feet farther.

"Kristen, are you okay?" Dad shouted.

This time, Mom tilted her head up without moving her body. She saw Morgan, James, and Dad peering down with horrified looks on their faces.

"I don't know," Mom managed to reply between breaths, then she dropped her head back down.

"Were you stung?" James shouted, thinking of the most dangerous animal in the park. *Is Mom having breathing difficulties?* he wondered.

Again Mom tried to get some traction. She slowly propped herself on her knees and dug a foot into the rocks, preparing to get up.

Morgan, James, and Dad saw Mom grimace in pain as she started to stand.

Finally, Mom put some weight on her back foot. She stood up, but the rocks gave out, sending Mom back to the ground and carrying her down the chute several more feet.

"I'll come get you!" Dad shouted. "Wait there!"

Again Mom peered upward. "You can't," she said, in obvious distress. "Then we'll both be stuck, and hurt."

Dad took a small step down into the chute anyway.
Immediately the rocks gave way, and he began to slide.

"Whoa!" Dad called out. He whirled around and lunged for the trail. James grabbed Dad's arm, and Morgan also gripped him. Then, slowly, Dad wormed his way back onto the path and stood up. He peered down at the chute, watching several tiny rocks roll toward Mom before stopping a few feet short of her. Dad guided Morgan and James back a few feet. "I'd be more comfortable if we stayed away from the edge."

Then Dad turned to Mom. "I can't get down there," he called out.

Surprisingly, Mom stood up again.

"How's your breathing?" James yelled down.

Mom looked up.

"We don't know if you're allergic or not," James explained.

Mom touched her cheek and her forehead. "Ow!" She flinched while yanking her hand away. *I'm bleeding*, she realized.

Morgan, James, and Dad peered down at Mom helplessly. Her pants were torn, and she appeared to be favoring one arm.

Mom looked up at her family. "Let me try climbing," she called up to them.

Mom took a few steps up the scree slope. Morgan, James, and Dad watched her nervously.

Mom made it up several feet. That's where the chute steepened. She dug her heel into the loose rocks until it felt firm. Then Mom rocked forward, trying to give herself some momentum. But her footing gave out, and she slid back down.

Once the latest cascade of rocks settled, Mom looked back up. "I don't know what to do," she said. "And my arm is killing me," she finally admitted.

The Parkers heard some clanking.

"Something's coming!" James called out.

Then they heard voices. Several people were crossing the avalanche chute. As the three hikers got closer, the Parkers saw they were carrying bulky backpacks with climbing equipment attached to the outside. The last person was wearing a red jacket.

"It's the mountaineers!" Morgan exclaimed.

The climbers carefully worked their way across the last section of blown-out trail. They looked over and saw Morgan, James, and Dad standing there with panicked, helpless looks on their faces.

Morgan noticed that the person in front was limping.

Dad guided the twins back another step to give the mountaineers some room. Finally the climbers reached the Parkers.

The person in front was shivering. He hobbled off the faint path and onto the main trail. The second climber quickly followed him. Then the woman with the red jacket approached. "Boy, it's good to get that over with again," she said.

"We have an emergency," Dad spoke up. "My wife fell down the chute."

The woman turned her gaze to where Morgan and James were looking and saw Mom. "What happened?"

James described the fall. "And she can't climb out," he finished.

"I can see why," the woman responded. She scanned the avalanche chute and the area nearby. Then she peered down the chute again, gauging its steepness. The woman walked several feet to the side and took a step into the slide area. She pulled her foot out just as a mini-avalanche of rocks trickled down. "That won't work," she said.

Immediately, the woman took off her backpack and pulled out her rope and some climbing gear. Then she looked at the people she was with. "How are you two doing?" she asked.

The climber in front checked the sky. It had begun to mist down rain. "I'm cold," he replied. "And my ankle is hurting."

"Do you two want to continue on to Elk Lake on your own?" the guide asked. "The other group is waiting there."

"Okay," the injured man nodded. "Should we send help?"

The woman looked at Mom. "I'm going to try to get her out. But I'll radio down to the other guide if I need assistance." The two climbers slowly trudged away.

"He fell into a crevasse on the glacier," the woman explained. "We're lucky we got him out of there with just a twisted ankle."

Then she looked at Dad. "I work for a mountaineering organization. I often lead trips onto Mount Olympus and its glaciers."

"Were you practicing on Hurricane Ridge last week?" James asked.

"Yes. I need to teach proper ice-climbing skills before we head up to the high peaks. Hurricane Ridge is a good place to practice."

"I thought I recognized you," James said.

The guide stood up with her rope. "I'm Cynthia," she said.

Cynthia walked over to a large tree in the slide area and dropped her pack next to it. She pulled out some webbing and looped it around the tree. Cynthia secured one end of the rope into the webbing and quickly put a rock-climbing harness around her legs and waist. Then she worked the rope through a device on her harness.

Cynthia took out a hand radio and called the climbing guide down at Elk Lake. She told him what had happened and described the rescue procedure. "I'll have the family call you if anything goes wrong," she finally said.

Then Cynthia handed the radio to Dad and showed him how to use it. "If I get hurt, call in right away," Cynthia said. "But I'm confident everything will be okay."

Cynthia looked below toward Mom and called out, "I'm coming down!" She turned backward and lowered herself into the chute.

Cynthia slowly let out more rope while touching her feet lightly on the unstable slope along the way.

Finally Cynthia made it within several feet to one side of Mom. She let out some slack in her rope and side-stepped over.

Mom and Cynthia talked for a moment, and they quickly looked over Mom's injuries. Then Cynthia looped the end of her rope around Mom several times and tied it securely. "Walk to the left," Cynthia instructed. "I'll be right behind you."

Mom took a deep breath and glanced sideways toward the forest. She looked over her shoulder at Cynthia. "Okay, here goes."

Mom sidestepped toward the trees while Cynthia followed her, keeping the rope taut. Slowly Mom moved closer to the edge of the avalanche chute.

As Mom and Cynthia traversed sideways, loose piles of rock continued to trickle out from underneath them. But they managed to keep their footing. Soon Mom reached the edge of the chute.

Cynthia watched Mom. "Go ahead, climb out now," she guided her.

Mom took another step sideways, holding onto the rope with her good arm for balance. She dug her feet into the rocks, gingerly crept onto the torn cliff, and scrambled over a series of exposed roots. Slowly Mom worked her way out of the avalanche area and into the forest below the trail.

"Yay!" Morgan called out.

Mom grabbed onto a tree and pulled herself several feet away from the slide. She sat down and held her arm.

Dad noticed the expression on Mom's face. "She's definitely hurting," he said to Morgan and James.

Meanwhile, Cynthia scrambled over to Mom. Then she undid the rope and put it aside. "I'm going to help you hike up to the trail now," she told Mom.

Cynthia judged the steep hillside. "I recommend that we grab on to tree roots and plants along the way."

Morgan, James, and Dad anxiously watched Cynthia and Mom crawl up through the forest. Mom held her right arm close to her body and tried not to move it as she worked her way toward the trail.

Dad stepped down and gave Mom a hand up for the final few steps. Then Morgan and James came over to hug her.

Mom flinched. "Ow!" she called out.

Dad looked at Mom's facial cuts, torn clothes, and the awkward way she stood. "We need to get you to a doctor," he said with concern.

Mom walked away from the slide area. She pulled out a jacket and tried to put it on. "Can you help me?" she said through chattering teeth. James held Mom's arm steady enough to get it through the sleeve of the jacket. "Thanks," Mom said, then she looked at the gray, misty sky. "Let's get to camp."

Cynthia and the Parkers all began hiking toward Elk Lake.

"I guess you aren't allergic to wasps," James said to Mom. "It's been over twenty minutes."

Mom tried to smile. "I guess not," she agreed.

Dad saw Elk Lake far below. "Almost there," he announced.

As they approached camp, the Parkers noticed the mountaineers gathered around a small fire. A lit lantern was nearby.

Mom walked toward the light. "Let's check my injuries here," she suggested.

Cynthia fished through her backpack and quickly pulled out a first-aid kit.

Dad and Cynthia began cleaning Mom's cuts and dabbing them with antiseptic. Mom flinched as they doctored her. Then Mom motioned to her arm. "We better take a look at this, too."

Dad gently pulled up Mom's sleeve. Her arm was badly scraped but not bleeding. But the area between Mom's elbow and wrist was red and swollen. Mom tried to bend her elbow. "It's stiffening up," she reported through clenched teeth.

Cynthia carefully folded a splint onto Mom's forearm. "I want to stabilize your arm to keep it from moving," she explained. Then Cynthia pulled out a sling and helped work Mom's arm into it. Once Cynthia was finished, Mom thanked her, then stood up. "We should get to camp before it's completely dark."

"I would feel more comfortable if you hiked out with us in the morning," Cynthia stated.

The Parkers looked at the mountaineers drinking warm soup. One of them had his ankle wrapped. He was bundled up, but still shivering.

"It looks like you have your own situation to deal with," Dad said. "But yes, we'll be here in the morning."

Dad led the way to camp. He quickly got the food down from the bear wires and hastily prepared dinner.

"Can you get me the ibuprofen, please?" Mom asked Morgan and James. "I'm really hurting."

After a quick dinner, the family shuffled into

their tent and got out of the rain. Once inside, Mom lay down, resting her injured arm on her stomach. A few moments later, Morgan pulled out her journal.

Dear Diary,

Today we just watched two groups of mountaineers climbing down from the icy summit of Mount Olympus. They have to use special gear like ice axes, ropes, and crampons on their shoes for gripping the ice. They also use the rope to tie themselves together in case one of them falls into a crevasse. Some of those crevasses we saw are deep. I don't know how they'd get out of one.

It's a good thing that they had a rope with them, because they ended up needing it and we did, too, to rescue Mom.

I'm not sure if our rescue of Mom is over, though. She's safely out of the avalanche chute, but we still have a long hike to our car, and then it's a long drive to town. I have a feeling that's where we're going, so we can get Mom to a doctor.

So far, though, Mom's insisting on walking out. Hopefully tomorrow's weather will make it a little easier, but we're not counting on it.

Anxiously reporting from the Olympics,

Morgan

Morgan closed her journal and turned toward Mom. "You're shivering!" she exclaimed.

"I know," Mom replied. "I've been cold since the fall. And it hurts to turn my body like I normally do to keep warm when I sleep."

Dad draped a flannel shirt over Mom, then nudged closer to her. Morgan did the same from the other side. "That should help," Mom said while managing a small smile. "Just be careful of my arm."

The family lay there, listening to the rain. As the night wore on, they drifted in and out of sleep.

• • •

The morning light gradually brightened the inside of the tent. Dad flicked on his headlamp and glanced at his watch. "It's already 7:30," he announced.

Mom turned her head toward Dad. "The clouds and forest are keeping it dark."

"What do you want to do?" Dad asked.

Mom lifted her injured arm slightly and thought for a moment. "Hike out," she answered. "At least as far as I can."

Mom watched as Morgan, James, and Dad slowly got up. They put on warm, dry clothes and helped Mom into hers. Finally, the family stuffed their sleeping bags into sacks and left the tent.

Once outside, Morgan and James quickly packed up the tent and backpacks while Dad retrieved the food. They munched on some dried fruit and nuts.

Dad grabbed Mom's backpack. He took out all her clothes and supplies and handed some to James and Morgan, keeping the rest. They stuffed Mom's belongings into their packs. Then Dad folded up Mom's pack and tied it onto the outside of his. "It's nice that your pack doesn't have a frame," he mentioned. "I can carry it with mine."

A few minutes later, the Parkers were ready to go. They walked over to the group of mountaineers. Cynthia was cooking breakfast while the

In case of emergency.

others were still resting in their sleeping bags.

"How are you this morning?" Cynthia asked Mom.

Mom sighed. "I think I can manage to walk out, with the help of ibuprofen anyway. It's probably better to do that than wait it out in the cold. I'm afraid I'd stiffen up."

Cynthia looked at Mom. "I'm happy to hear that. Rescues can be a difficult and lengthy ordeal in the rain forest and mountains. But we'll follow you out. Plus, there's a ranger on duty at Olympus Guard Station," she said, "and a hospital in Forks."

"Thanks," Dad replied.

The first part of the trail was downhill and soggy from the rain. Mom trudged along carefully while James, Morgan, and Dad kept her pace.

The family walked in silence, their thoughts focused on Mom's arm and the day ahead.

"It's a good thing we brought our rain gear," Morgan eventually said, shaking water off the hood of her poncho.

They continued on, crossing over the small bridge at Martin's Creek then returning to the two deep gorges of cascading glacial meltwater.

Mom stopped and looked down from the bridge. "Let me rest a minute," she said while staring at the gray water.

James also gazed into the gorge. "Does the water level seem higher?"

The Parkers studied the two creeks, comparing them to what they remembered. "It sure sounds louder," Dad said.

"Do you think it's raining or snowing on top of the glacier now?" James asked.

"Probably raining," Dad replied. "It's summer, and that could be feeding these streams."

Dad pulled out four energy bars. "You guys have to be hungry," he said and passed them out.

The Parkers trekked on while eating. Soon they passed the campsite marker at 12.4 miles. After that the trail leveled out. "I think that's it for the downhill," Mom recalled.

"How's your arm?" Dad asked.

Mom glanced at her sling. "When I keep it still, it's not too bad," she reported.

Eventually, the family passed Lewis Meadow and kept going until they reached Olympus Guard Station, around noon.

The Parkers walked into the shelter to get out of the rain. They sat down, and Dad quickly started boiling a pot of water. The family ate a late breakfast of hot oatmeal with dried fruit. Mom took some more ibuprofen.

While they were eating, the backcountry ranger walked in. "How are you all?" he asked.

"Okay, considering," Dad said, glancing at Mom.

The ranger looked at Mom's sling. "And how's your arm?"

"I'm managing," Mom replied. "Did you hear something about it?"

"Word travels quickly out here." The ranger held up his radio. "The mountaineers will be along shortly."

The Parkers began packing up the stove and dishes.

"What's the weather report today?" Dad asked.

"It was just called in," the ranger responded. "More rain the next two days."

Just then, Cynthia's group walked up. "Hi," she said, greeting them. Mom looked at the climbers. One of them was still limping.

"We should keep moving," Mom said, "while we're at least somewhat warm and dry."

"I'll be hiking out to the Hoh Visitor Center later today," the ranger said. "If you need to stop and camp, please put a sign at the mile marker where there is a trail leading to a backcountry campsite. That way I can

Ranger on duty here.

check on you and call in to the permit office that you are using that spot. We'd also like you to fill out an incident report when you can."

The Parkers continued their trek out. The sky was brighter, but it was still raining. In the lower elevations, Morgan, James, Mom, and Dad felt a little bit warmer. James called out mile marker signs as they passed them, noting their progress. Finally James announced, "Happy Four Campsite, only 5.7 miles left."

• • •

It was late afternoon when the family stopped at the 2.9-mile signpost. "It's 5 PM," Dad announced. Then he looked at Mom. "What do you want to do?"

Mom leaned against a tree and thought briefly. "We're making decent time on this flat trail. I would rather get to the car than camp out here in the rain."

"Can you two continue on?" Dad asked Morgan and James.

The twins nodded.

They walked on, eventually working their way back onto the Spruce Nature Trail. "I don't think we can go check your stick right now," Mom said to James. "Sorry about that."

James shrugged his shoulders, then smiled at Mom. "It's okay."

"I bet the rain has raised the water level, though," Dad said.

"I bet you're right," James replied.

Soon they were back at the visitor center. Dad walked up to it and peered inside. "It's closed," he announced.

Morgan pointed to a sign by the door. "What about this? 'In case of an emergency, please call 911.'"

Dad dialed the number at the pay phone and explained to the dispatch person what had happened. Then he hung up the phone.

"A ranger is going to meet us at the hospital," Dad informed his family. "Let's get going."

The Parkers walked over to the car, threw their gear haphazardly into the trunk, and piled in. Mom grimaced as she squirmed into the front seat. Dad leaned over and buckled her seat belt.

Dad started the engine and cranked up the heat. "We'll be in town soon enough," he announced.

They drove out of the rain forest and passed the park entrance station.

Dad continued driving. At a junction, he turned

north. A while later they arrived in the town of Forks. Dad slowed down as they passed several stores and hotels.

Dad stopped at a hotel and dashed inside to ask if a room was available and how to get to the hospital. Then he jogged back to the car. "It's just a few blocks away," he announced.

"Are there rooms?" Mom asked.

"Yes, we'll be able to stay here tonight."

• • •

Dad made a turn, then found the hospital. He parked the car and ran around to open Mom's door. Dad helped Mom out, and the family escorted her to the emergency room.

"I'm really hurting," Mom groaned.

Once they were inside, Mom and Dad described the incident to the admitting clerk. She asked them some questions and typed the answers into the computer.

"I think my arm might be broken," Mom said.

"And we might want to take a look at her other injuries," Dad added, referring to Mom's cuts and scrapes.

"Okay, have a seat and a nurse will call you back," the clerk said.

Mom gently sat in a chair. Dad draped a thick coat around her and brushed her hair back from her face.

A few minutes later, a nurse appeared. "Kristen Parker," she called.

Mom and Dad stood up. Dad glanced at Morgan and James. "I'll be right back." Dad looked at the admitting clerk. "Can you keep an eye on the kids for me?"

The woman nodded. Then Dad followed Mom into the emergency room.

• • •

A few minutes later, Dad returned to the waiting room. Morgan and James were there with the ranger, who had just walked into the room. They all stood up. "How's Mom?" Morgan asked.

"They're not sure yet," Dad replied. "They're taking X-rays right now."

The family reported the incident to the ranger. Then the ranger looked at Morgan, James, and Dad. "Wasps can sure cause a lot of problems for something so small," she said. "But we're still going to have the backcountry ranger assess that part of the trail to see if it's safe for crossing. We don't want to take the chance of anyone else getting hurt out there."

The ranger finished writing down information on a form, then put away her pen. "We'll get the report of Kristen's injuries from the hospital," she said.

After saying good-bye to the ranger, Dad looked at Morgan and James. "They did say that Mom might be here for a few hours. I know we're still in wet clothes and we haven't eaten much all day." Dad paused for a moment. "Do you want to check in at the hotel, get changed, and grab something to eat?"

James looked at Dad. "What about Mom?"

"It's her idea," Dad replied. "Besides," Dad held up his cell phone, "we get reception here, and it's a small town. We'll only be a few blocks away."

Morgan, James, and Dad walked to the car.

Dad drove to the hotel, and after checking in, they unloaded their gear, quickly changed, and drove to the supermarket. Morgan, James, and Dad picked up food for the next couple of days.

Once they returned to the hotel and brought in the groceries, Dad's cell phone rang.

"Hi, honey. How are you?" he said.

Dad listened for a minute.

"I'm sorry," Dad said.

Then he listened some more.

"How are you feeling now?"

"Okay, absolutely, we can do that. See you in a few minutes, sweetie."

• • •

Dad hung up the phone. He walked over to a desk and opened it, pulling out a phone book.

"What did the doctor say?" Morgan asked.

"Mom was right. She broke her arm," Dad reported. "They're putting a cast on it now. But other than that, she's going to be okay."

Dad started flipping through the phone book.

"What are you looking for?" James asked.

"They're putting her on pain medication for the next few days," Dad explained. "We'll need to stop at the pharmacy tomorrow and pick that up. But," Dad found the section on restaurants, "Mom says she's really hungry and wants to know if we can get a pizza."

Morgan and James looked at each other approvingly.

Dad called the pizzeria. "Yes, a large, with all the toppings," he ordered. Then Dad listened. "We'll be there in thirty minutes."

Dad hung up the phone then glanced at Morgan and James. "Come on, let's go get Mom."

They left the hotel and drove back to the hospital. Morgan, James, and Dad hurried inside. Mom was sitting in the waiting room with her arm in a cast and sling. She also had a large gauze bandage on her forehead and a small one on her cheek.

"Mom!" James called out while running over to greet her.

Morgan and Dad hurried over too. Mom looked at her family and smiled. She gestured toward her injured arm. "You can be the first ones to sign my cast!"

Dad smiled at Mom. "First let's get you to the hotel. You look tired."

"It's been a long day," Mom admitted. "And the pain medication is making me groggy." Mom looked at her family. "Where's dinner?"

Dad helped Mom to her feet. "It's waiting for us," he replied.

Morgan, James, and Dad helped Mom to the car. They drove to the pizza parlor. Dad dashed in and paid for dinner. He hurried back to the car and hopped in with the take-out box.

Mom smelled the pizza. "Now I'm really hungry," she said.

Dad drove the family back to the hotel. Once inside, they sprawled out on the beds, ate pizza, and watched an old rerun of a family movie on TV.

• • •

Late the next morning, James got out of bed and grabbed a banana from one of their grocery bags. He walked over to the window, pulled the drapes back, and peeked outside. "It's still raining," he reported between bites of the fruit.

Dad got up and gathered their wet, dirty clothes together. Morgan and James jumped up and helped. "We might as well get some laundry done while we're here," Dad said. "We'll be right back," he told Mom.

• • •

Dad and the twins put the clothes into the washing machine. Dad placed coins in the slots. "Mom's a real trouper," Dad said. "I don't know if I could have hiked all that way with a broken arm."

When they returned, Mom was lying in bed with her eyes closed. "I think she's asleep," Morgan whispered.

Mom mumbled a pretend snore. Then a big smile spread across her face. Morgan and James came over and sat next to Mom on the bed.

Dad also walked up. "How does it feel to have us take care of you for a change?"

"Maybe I'll have to break my arm more often," Mom replied.

Dad laughed. "No, don't. We need you healthy!"

Mom looked at her family. "I do feel better," she reported. "But, obviously, long hikes or backpacking are out for me for the rest of this trip. Still," Mom mused, "I don't want to go home. Olympic is way too beautiful to leave."

Mom glanced at the map and guidebook lying on the hotel room desk. "Can the three of you find something that all of us can do on our last day here tomorrow?"

"Deal!" Dad exclaimed.

Morgan, James, and Dad walked over to the desk. They unfolded the map and studied it. Then they pored over the book.

"What about this area?" James suggested.

"Yeah, we haven't even seen that part of the park," Dad agreed. "Good idea."

Dad read a bit more. He found a phone number and dialed it on his cell phone. Dad walked outside the hotel room. "For better reception," he explained.

A few minutes later, Dad came back in. "Okay," he reported, "we're all set."

"Now all we have to hope for is dry weather," Mom said.

"Speaking of dry," James realized, "the clothes should be ready for the dryer now."

• • •

The rest of the day, the Parkers stayed in their hotel room, finished their laundry, read, napped, and watched more TV. Later, Dad picked up another pizza for dinner.

In the morning, the Parkers took their time

packing up. Eventually, they left the hotel and the town of Forks. The family drove south on Highway 101, heading to another part of the park.

Before reaching their destination, Dad pulled the car over at a sign that said Beach 4. "Here's our first stop for the day," he announced.

The Parkers joined a group of people gathered in a parking lot. "Welcome to the other part of the Olympics," a ranger said to the group. "I'm Ranger Darrel. Today we're going to walk to a place where there is more wildlife than any other location in the park. Follow me."

Darrel led the group on a short trail toward the beach. At the edge of the sand, he turned and faced everyone. "See that stack of rocks over there?" He pointed. "That's where the stars really come out."

Darrel added, "There are sea creatures out there eating at an outdoor restaurant. You'll see."

The group followed Darrel toward the shore. On the way, he strolled up to the Parkers. "Are you the family who just came down from Blue Glacier?"

"You know too?" James asked.

"National parks are like family," he explained. "We all hear what's going on." Then Darrel looked at Mom's cast. "How's the arm doing?"

"Oh, it doesn't feel too bad," Mom said. "And in six weeks, when the cast is off, I'm supposed to make a full recovery."

"That's good to hear," Darrel replied. "From what I was told, the mishap could have been much worse."

Darrel stopped by a dead crab and picked it up. "If you've been on the beach at all around here, you've probably seen one of these." He held the crab out.

"They're all over the place," James commented.

Darrel smiled. "And you might be wondering what's killing them, right? Well, they're not dead! What you've been seeing are shells the crabs have outgrown. When that happens, they crawl out of their shell and hide

for a few days so predators don't find a nice, soft, easy meal. They stay in hiding until they grow new shells."

Darrel tossed the shell on the sand and continued walking. "Interesting, isn't it?"

Finally, they reached the edge of the tide pools.

Darrel hopped onto a rock and waited for the group near a clear pool. Dad helped Mom across.

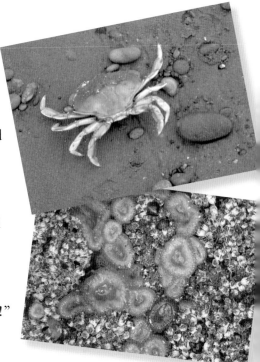

The visitors gazed into the water. "Wow!" Dad exclaimed. "Look at all those!"

"Those," Darrel interjected, "are sea anemones. And some can live for over a hundred years."

The group gazed at the unusual creatures as their colorful tentacles drifted gently with the current.

"It's the giant green ones that live the longest," Darrel explained. "Those smaller purplish ones that are bunched together," he said, pointing, "they're actually reproductions. They clone themselves."

Darrel scanned the group. "I need a brave volunteer."

Morgan slowly raised her hand.

"Perfect," Darrel said. "Come on up!"

Morgan stepped forward.

"Can you tell us your name, young lady?" Darrel asked.

"Morgan. Morgan Parker."

"And where are you from?"

"San Luis Obispo, California."

"Great. San Luis Obispo. A beautiful coastal town. So you know all about the ocean, right?"

Morgan nodded her head tentatively.

Darrel pointed into the pool. "Have you ever felt one of those?"

"No," Morgan answered.

"Do you want to?"

Morgan looked unsure. "I guess I volunteered, didn't I?"

"Yes, you did," Darrel said playfully. "Step down and try touching the inside of one of those large green sea anemones."

Morgan knelt down and extended her hand. She lifted a finger toward the sea anemone and slowly moved it closer. Morgan glanced back at Mom and Dad.

Quickly, Morgan touched the inside of the tide pool creature.

The sea anemone closed up around Morgan's finger. Morgan yanked her hand away and stood up with a startled look on her face.

"How did it feel?" Mom asked.

Morgan thought for a second. "Kind of spongy and kind of sticky."

"It's a good thing you pulled your hand out of there," Darrel said. "Do you know why?"

Morgan looked at Darrel.

"Because in a few weeks or so it would have digested your whole hand."

Morgan wiped her hand on her jacket. She clenched her fist and released it, then glanced at her intact fingers.

"Generally," Darrel explained, "sea creatures should be left undisturbed. But I wanted to show you, just on this talk, what it is like to touch one. Come on," Darrel added, "let's take a look at the big show."

The group followed him across several more tidal rocks. "There are starfish everywhere!" James noticed.

Darrel stopped. "From here you can see why this place is called Starfish Point." He looked all around. "How many do you think we can see right now?"

The group scanned the tide pools.

Finally James called out, "There are too many to count!"

Darrel smiled. "Yes, that's probably true. But we estimate well over one hundred starfish can be seen from right here."

Darrel waited to let the group view the starfish. Then he went on. "Starfish are also called sea stars. They are part of a family called echinoderms. *Echinoderm* means hard, scaly skin, which certainly describes a starfish.

"Does anyone know another type of living thing that fits in this category?" Darrel asked.

"Sea urchins," someone called out.

"Sea urchins is correct!" Darrel exclaimed. "As well as sand dollars, which are sometimes seen on our beaches.

"Sea stars," Darrel continued, "really know how to go out for a meal, what we would call a take-out dinner. They clamp themselves over their favorite food, a mussel. The starfish slowly pries the shell apart while sliding its stomach into the mussel. Then the starfish digests the mussel in its own shell before pulling its stomach back in."

Darrel smiled at the group. "How's that for going out to eat?"

James looked at all the starfish. He noticed one with a shorter leg. "Can starfish really lose their legs and grow new ones?" he asked.

"An excellent question!" Darrel replied. "Yes, they can, and sometimes I've seen uneven-legged starfish around here."

"There's one over there," James pointed.

"Indeed, there is," Darrel responded, then he looked at the group. "This is the end of our guided walk. Take your time and explore some more. If you have any questions, I'll be hanging out for a while. Thank you for coming to Beach 4's Starfish Point."

The group clapped.

Morgan, James, Mom, and Dad looked around a little longer. Eventually, the Parkers left the tide pools and drove to Kalaloch Campground, their last stop in the park.

The Parkers drove into Kalaloch Campground.

They found their assigned site, A-46, and started setting up. "I love it," Mom declared. "Camping in the forest yet right next to the beach."

Dad started putting wood into the fire pit. "So it's ready for later," he explained.

"How about for now?" Mom asked. "It's so cool and foggy out."

Dad lit the fire. Then James pulled up a chair for Mom and got her book for her. Morgan dashed to the car and grabbed a spare blanket.

Mom sat down, and Morgan wrapped the blanket around her. "I think I'll hang out a bit, if all of you don't mind," Mom said.

"Of course," Dad replied. "We're going to walk to the store and get a few things. Do you need anything?"

"I'm good now, thanks," Mom answered.

Morgan, James, and Dad followed a path to the store. The twins each bought a kite, and Dad got supplies for dinner. Then they headed back.

Once they put their food away, James put another log on the fire for Mom. She smiled at James. "Thanks."

Morgan, James, and Dad said good-bye to Mom.

They trekked through a thickly forested trail toward the beach.

"It's like a giant rabbit hole in here," James mentioned.

"Or a plant tunnel," Morgan added.

"I was thinking gnome land," Dad said.

At the end of the trail, an opening in the plants led to the ocean. Morgan, James, and Dad stepped up to the clearing.

They hopped across giant driftwood logs until they reached the sand. Then Dad led Morgan and James through a series of stretches. Afterward, he stood up and gazed at the vast, flat, open shoreline. "Jogging on the beach!" Dad exclaimed. "And with my children, I love it!"

They took off, heading north.

• • •

Morgan, James, and Dad approached a series of rocks and slowed down. Dad noticed a path up to the top of the rocks. He helped Morgan and James climb up. They stood on their natural platform and gazed out at the miles of ocean and shoreline.

"We better get back now," Dad said, and the three of them hopped down from the rocks and began jogging toward camp.

• • •

Mom turned a page in her book and glanced at her watch. *An hour?* she thought. *Wow, that's quite a jog!*

Mom got up and stretched out her sore muscles. She doused the fire with water and took the forested trail toward the beach.

• • •

"There's our rabbit hole," James said, pointing it out. Morgan, James, and Dad stopped running.

"Wait a minute," Dad said as he leaned over. "That was quite a run. I need to catch my breath."

Morgan noticed a wood structure set up in the sand. "It's a little fortress," she called out.

Morgan and James walked up to the fort. "Let's fix it up," Morgan suggested. Dad joined them. They reinforced the walls with more planks of wood. Soon, three sides of the fort were complete. "We can leave this last wall open," Morgan said, "for our door."

Then Dad started digging out a fire pit.

James stepped out of the fortress and looked at it from the outside. "It looks pretty cool," he said. James found several pieces of old rope and a broken buoy that had washed up on shore. He tied the decorations onto the fort's walls, then gazed at their creation proudly.

A movement near the forest caught James's eye. He turned and saw Mom at the top of the trail. She was waving James over.

James waved back. "Mom's over there," he said.

The twins and Dad jogged over to Mom and helped her across the giant logs. They led her to the fort. "Make yourself at home," Dad said.

Mom gazed at their creation. "It looks like you've been busy." She slowly sat down in the sand.

Dad rubbed Mom's back. "Would you like to have dinner out here?"

"Sure," Mom replied.

• • •

Morgan, James, and Dad trekked back to camp and picked up supplies. They returned to the shelter and began setting up. Then Dad hiked back to the car once more. "I forgot something," he said.

Dad grabbed his guitar out of the car and played a few chords. He spent a few minutes tuning it. When he returned to the beach, Morgan and James had their kites high in the air.

Dad walked up to Morgan. "You sure got that up there quickly."

"It was really easy," Morgan replied. She gazed at her colorful kite. "The wind just lifted it right off the ground."

Dad walked over to James and looked at his kite. The breeze whipped it around. "How's it going?" Dad asked.

"It's a strong wind," James reported. "But I can hold onto it."

Dad returned to the fort and helped Mom get a fire started. They set up their beach chairs and hung out, watching Morgan and James.

A while later, Morgan let her kite sink to the ground. She reeled in the string, then brought the kite into the shelter.

Morgan grabbed her daypack and pulled out her journal. She sat in one of their chairs and started writing:

Dear Diary,

The sun is beginning to set on our trip. But we are in no hurry to make dinner. Evenings move slowly here in the north. It won't be completely dark until almost 10 p.m.

It's funny how Mom's injuries changed our plans. But I really can't think of a better way to spend our last day here. It's been great just hanging out at the beach.

Olympic is like three parks in one. There's the high peaks and glaciers, the rain forest, and, where we're at now, the ocean. I'm not sure what part I like best, and it shows on my top ten list. So here goes:

1. Klahane Ridge Trail
2. Camping at the beach
3. Sol Duc Hot Springs
4. Sol Duc Falls
5. Hurricane Ridge wildflowers and views
6. Heart O' the Hills campground
7. Elwha River Valley and old cabins
8. The bear climbing the snow at Hurricane Ridge
9. Hall of Mosses Trail and Rain Forest
10. Blue Glacier!

There are so many places here that we didn't get to see. I'll remember Staircase, Enchanted Valley, and the High Divide for next time.

Until then,

Morgan

James walked into the shelter with his kite. He saw Morgan's journal. "My turn," he announced.

This is James Parker reporting.

I love glaciers! And I can't wait to see some more.

Dad and I looked at a US map yesterday, trying to figure out where else they are. It turns out that here in Washington, we are in "Glacier Central." There are huge glaciers nearby at Mount Rainier, and a bunch in the North Cascades. But Oregon's mountains have some as well, and so does California, although they're much smaller there. Maybe soon we'll go to Glacier National Park in Montana. Dad says the glaciers there are melting and only have a few years left.

What are my favorite sites in Olympic? Many of them are about glaciers.

1. Blue Glacier and its cracks

2. Iceberg chunks and other glaciers near Mount Olympus

3. Metallic-colored water on the Blue Glacier Trail

4. White Glacier view on the trail

5. Walking to the beach on the boardwalk through the forest

6. Rock drawings on the beach

7. Starfish Point!

8. Hurricane Ridge views

9. Hall of Mosses Trail

10. Rope climbing on the beach

When I come back to Olympic, I want to do it as a mountaineer. I can't imagine anything more exciting then scaling Mount Olympus's icy summit. And, there are over 60 glaciers in this park, so there's plenty to explore here.

Reporting from Olympic,

James Parker

James closed his journal and looked up. Mom turned over her hot dog and cooked the other side. "Aren't you hungry?" she asked James.

James put a hot dog on a skewer and started roasting it.

Dad finished eating his hot dog and leaned back in his chair. "How can we top this trip?" he asked with satisfaction.

"It's going to be hard to return to the real world," Mom added.

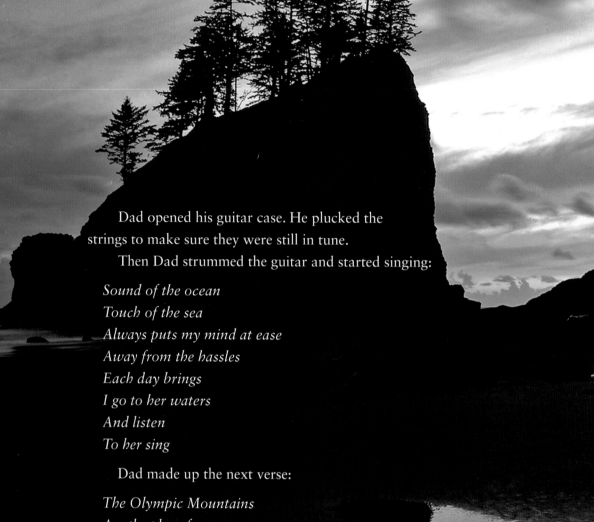

Dad opened his guitar case. He plucked the strings to make sure they were still in tune.

Then Dad strummed the guitar and started singing:

Sound of the ocean
Touch of the sea
Always puts my mind at ease
Away from the hassles
Each day brings
I go to her waters
And listen
To her sing

Dad made up the next verse:

The Olympic Mountains
Are the place for me
Cracking blue glaciers
And rivers roaming free
Miles of wilderness
And wild ocean sands
Moss-draped rain forests
Are abundant, in this land…